W9-BMZ-583

SITWE JOSEPH GOES TO SCHOOL

Story by
Twesigye Jackson Kaguri

Art by
Obol Andrew Jackson

Sitwe Joseph Goes to School by Twesigye Jackson Kaguri

Art by Obol Andrew Jackson

Special thanks to Susan Urbanek Linville

Published by Nyaka AIDS Orphans Project, PO Box 339, East Lansing, MI 48826

ISBN-13:978-1497425538

ISBN-10:1497425530

DEDICATION

To all current and past Nyaka and Kutamba students: I am inspired by your determination, resilience, and hard work.

To all children around the world who have no opportunity to attend school: Stay strong. You are not forgotten.

To Tabitha, my wife, Nicolas & Nolan, my sons, and Talia & Tessa, my twin daughters: You mean the world to me. I would not be able to do what I do without your support, your love, and your smiles.

A special thank you goes to Jon and Cathy Freeman for funding the initial publication of this book. All proceeds from sales will support Nyaka and Kutamba nursery programs.

Sitwe Joseph lay on a woven banana leaf mat in his mukaaka's small hut. Mornings were chilly in their mountain village. He and his younger brother, Stephen, huddled under Mukaaka's old gomesi dress. There was nothing in his little tummy to keep him warm.

"Sitwe," Mukaaka called from outside. "I know you are awake. Go gather firewood."

Sitwe sat up and rubbed his dry eyes. This was the day he would refuse to obey.

"Sitwe Joseph!"

Mukaaka crouched by an open fire. The sky was blue. She could cook without worry of rains washing the fire away. By midday, they would eat steamed matooke, cabbage, and maybe some beans.

"Komu will be back with water soon," Mukaaka said. "I need more wood."

Sitwe dared not look her in the eye. "I am going to school today," he said.

"I will not hear talk of school again," Mukaaka said.

"My other friends are going," he said. He had watched boys and girls of all ages in their light blue uniforms walking the dirt paths on their way to school. He and Komu and Stephen should be in school too.

Mukaaka braced herself on her walking stick and stood with a groan.

"You are not the others," she said. "They have parents who are alive, or an uncle who can afford to send them to school."

"I know," Sitwe said. "I am an orphan." He felt sad. He remembered his father's voice and rough hands. He did not remember his mother who died from HIV/AIDS when he was only two.

"I would send you to school if I could," Mukaaka said. "But I cannot even afford a pencil."

Sitwe walked between trees, gathering sticks to add to the fire. If only they had a chicken, they could sell eggs. Then they would have money to buy a pencil.

He thought about convincing one of Mr. Mugisha's chickens to follow him home. No. That was not right. That would be stealing.

A black crow landed in the tree above him and cawed. "School. School," it seemed to say.

"I am going to school," Sitwe said. "Today!"

Sitwe stacked his wood at the edge of a wide grassy path. Two girls in light blue uniforms talked and laughed as they walked by. They were going to school.

Sitwe looked left and right. Komu would return with the water soon, but she was not here now.

Sitwe could not resist. He would follow the girls.

The girls walked faster than Sitwe.
Soon, they were far ahead of him.

He followed the road past banana plantations and cassava fields. He saw houses. Some were like his own, made of sticks and mud with banana leaf roofing. Others were larger and made of brick with iron roofs.

Sitwe wanted a brick house. Rain would not drip through the holes. Malaria mosquitoes would not sneak in to bite him.

He imagined going to school to become a doctor. He would take care of Mukaaka when she became sick. He would buy her a goat, and a cow, and chickens. Lots of chickens.

The school sat at the top of a hill. The wooden window shutters were open. Sitwe rushed to the nearest window. He was too short to see inside.

He heard teachers giving instructions.

"We will practice addition," a teacher said. "One plus one equals two."

"Two plus one equals three," the teacher and class said together.

"Three plus one equals four."

Sitwe grabbed the window ledge and used his feet to climb up. Inside, a teacher pointed to a blackboard.

"Four plus one equals five," she said.

White marks were drawn on the blackboard. Sitwe wished he could read them.

"Four plus one equals five," he repeated with the class.

Startled, Sitwe dropped from the wall. He wanted to hide, but it was too late for that. Komu had already seen him. He walked slowly to his sister.

Komu set jerry cans on the ground. "Does Mukaaka know you are here?" she said.

"No."

"Just as I thought," she said. "You are in big trouble."

"Please, don't tell," Sitwe said. "I just wanted to go to school."

"Get that out of your head," Komu said. "None of us can go to school. That is the way it is."

It was almost mid-day. Matooke steamed in a pot over the fire. Mukaaka shelled ground nuts and fed them to Stephen. Komu swept the dirt floor with a hand broom.

Sitwe's stomach growled, but he was too annoyed to be hungry. He must think of a way to go to school.

"Sitwe," Komu said. "Do not just sit there. Go ask Cousin Agaba if he has work for you in his banana plantation."

Sitwe frowned. He didn't want to work in the trees. He wanted to learn.

"Go," Mukaaka said. "Agaba's avocado tree is filled with fruit. He is sure to give us some."

"Yes, Mukaaka."

The sun was hot in Cousin Agaba's vegetable garden. Weeds stretched as far as Sitwe could see. Thirsty, Sitwe joined two older boys in the shade of a banana tree.

"Someday you will be strong enough to carry bananas like me," Benjamin said, flexing his muscles.

"No." Sitwe shook his head. "I am going to school. I want to be a doctor."

Benjamin laughed. "That's ridiculous. Orphans do not go to school."

"Some orphans do," Samuel said. He scratched a long scar on his arm. "There is a free AIDS orphans school in Nyakagyezi, near Kambuga Town."

"Kambuga town?" Sitwe had been there once. It wasn't far.

At the end of the day, Sitwe arrived at Mukaaka's house, breathless. He dropped a bag of vegetables inside the door.

"I have good news," he said. "There is an orphans school. It's free. They even have pencils."

Komu laughed. "Someone is telling you stories."

Mukaaka frowned. "I have never heard of such a thing."

"It's true," Sitwe said. "Dennis said they have purple uniforms. Samuel said it is near Kambuga."

"I want no more talk about schools," Mukaaka said. "You should not get your hopes up."

Sitwe could not sleep. He imagined walking to school with the other students, dressed in black shorts and a purple shirt.

Stop fidgeting,"Komu said from across the dark room.

"Can we go to Nyakagyezi?" Sitwe said.

"It is much too far for me to walk," Mukaaka said. "Even with your young legs, it would take half the morning to get there."

"I can run," Sitwe said.

"Go to sleep," Mukaaka said. "You can go to school in your dreams."

Sitwe lay awake all night. When birds began to sing, he knew morning was close. If he was going to find this free school, he would have to do it on his own.

Quietly, he crept from his mat and opened the single wooden door to their house. There was no sign of the sunrise, but he could find the road to Kambuga Town in darkness.

Sitwe's feet grew sore from walking the stony path. He expected to be in Kambuga soon, but the road continued past plantations, gardens, huts, and brick houses.

He came to a stony outcropping where water rushed down to the river far below. Sitwe was too short to jump the stream. If he fell in, he would be washed away.

"Caw," a crow called from a high tree. "Go home."

"Go away," he yelled. He waved his hands and the bird flew off.

Maybe he should turn back.

No. He must think of some way

Sitwe spied a branch near the rushing water. Using all his strength, he rolled it into the stream. Muddy water gurgled over the smooth bark.

The crow clacked its beak.

"You see," Sitwe said. "I made a bridge."

The crow chattered.

The crow took flight.

Sitwe tip-toed onto the branch. It bowed beneath him. Cold water rushed over his feet.

Sitwe slid.

"Oh no," he yelled.

Muddy water splashed his face and filled his mouth.

He held tightly to the branch.

"Help!"

There was no one there to help him.

"I will help myself," Sitwe said.

He struggled against the current and looped his legs around the branch.

Using all his strength, he inched along the branch.

He was going to make it to the school. Nothing could stop him.

Finally, Sitwe reached the other side and sat at the edge of the road. His face was wet. His clothes were soaked.

A red pickup truck with a bed full of people passed by. It threw dust and pebbles into the air. Sitwe covered his face. He would not give up. Kambuga was just beyond the next bend. He was sure of it.

There was no town beyond that bend or the next. Three crows sat high in a tree, clicking beaks and chattering.

"Where is the school?" Sitwe called.

They stared back at him.

"Stupid birds," he mumbled.

Maybe Mukaaka was right. The school was too far.

In the distance, Sitwe spied a bit of purple moving along the roadside.

Was it flowers?

Was it a uniform?

Sitwe forgot his tiredness and ran.

He approached a girl about Komu's age wearing a purple uniform. She paid no attention to him.

"Stop," he said.

She turned and gave him a puzzled look.

"Agandi," he greeted her.

"Nimarungi."

"I am looking for the free school," he said.

"Nyaka AIDS Orphans School?" she said.

"Yes" He breathed deep to catch his breath. "I am an AIDS orphan."

"Me too," she said. "I am walking there. My name is Christine."

"I am Sitwe," he said.

The school was more beautiful than Sitwe had imagined. Its buildings sat behind an iron gate. The walls were painted white and the shutters purple.

A white van was parked by the gate. Christine pointed to the words. "It says, Nyaka AIDS Orphans School," she said.

"I am here to learn to read," Sitwe said. "And become a doctor."

Christine laughed.

"I am not being funny," Sitwe said.

"I know." Christine pointed to one of the doors. "First you must apply to be a student. You must see the headmaster."

Sitwe went to the headmaster's office. "Who are you?" the man asked.

"I am Sitwe," he said. "I want to go to school."

"To become a Nyaka student, you must apply," the headmaster said. "And we do not have room for everyone who applies."

"I am an orphan," Sitwe said. "I live with my Mukaaka."

"We would need one hundred schools to educate all the orphans in Kanungu District," he said.

"But I *must* go to school," Sitwe said. "I *must* become a Doctor."

"You are a determined little boy," the headmaster said. "I will put you in the Nursery class for the morning. After lunch we will visit your mukaaka. "

"Thank you, Mr. Headmaster," Sitwe said.

Two months. The headmaster told them that was how long they would have to wait for a decision.

Sitwe walked to the main road every morning and looked for the white Nyaka van. Every day it did not come.

"Do not get your hopes up," Mukaaka said. "The school cannot take everyone."

Crows gathered in the trees to tease him. He threw stones at them.

"I am going to school," he said. "Leave me alone."

Sitwe was returning from the banana plantation
when he saw the Nyaka School van outside Mukaaka's
house. He ran as fast as he could.

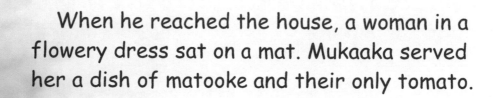

When he reached the house, a woman in a flowery dress sat on a mat. Mukaaka served her a dish of matooke and their only tomato.

"Am I going to school?" Sitwe asked. "Am I?"

"Remember your manners," Mukaaka said.

Sitwe nodded. "Agandi, Nyabo," he said.

"Nimarungi." The woman smiled. "Yes, you are going to school."

NYAKA AIDS ORPHANS SCHOOL

Sitwe lives in Uganda. Uganda is a small country in East Africa.

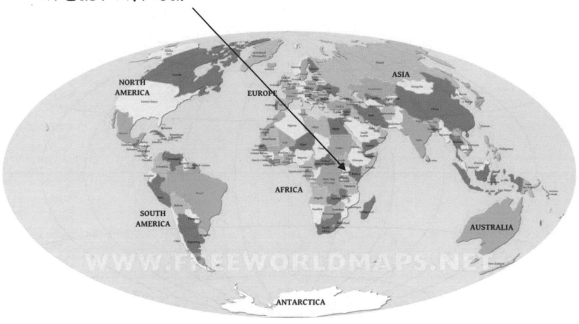

Uganda's flag has a bird on it. The bird is the Crested Crane. There are four crane species living in Africa. The Crested Crane is about 3 feet (100 cm) tall.

Bananas are a popular food in Uganda. There are many different types of bananas. Matooke bananas are picked from the tree when they are green. They are steamed and mashed before they are eaten.

Students cannot attend school in Uganda if they do not wear a uniform.

Uganda has 40 spoken languages. The Rukiga language that is used in this book is commonly spoken in Western Uganda.

Agandi means "How are you."
Nimarungi means "I am fine."
Mukaaka means "grandmother."

HELP MAKE A DIFFERENCE

Visit www.nyakaschool.org for more information about the Nyaka AIDS Orphans Project.

Become a Friend of the Nyaka on Facebook, or become Jackson's friend there. You can also follow Jackson on Twitter at twitter.com/twejaka.

If you want to read more, check out the book, *A School for My Village,* on Amazon or at your local bookstore or library.

Form a Friends of Nyaka Group or join one in your area. Our friends Groups help spread the message. Check out our web site to learn how you can start a group in your community.

Become a Young Hero for Nyaka. Some Young Heroes have gathered books, collected relative's pocket change, and dedicated birthday money for donation.

For more information:

Nyaka AIDS Orphans Project
PO Box 339
East Lansing, MI 48826
info@nyakaschool.org
(517) 575-6623

28238101R00033

Made in the USA
Charleston, SC
06 April 2014